This book belongs to

....

Front endpapers by Kathleen Yu aged 7 (left) and Marwin Himmelreich aged 7 (right)
Back endpapers by Pablo Rosa Garcia aged 8 (left) and Isabella Fantoni aged 7 (right)
A big thank you to the International School of Amsterdam, the Netherlands
for helping with the endpapers—K.P

For Sam and Natalie—V.T.
For Kate and Captain Jack—K.P.

OXFORD
UNIVERSITY PRESS

Great Clarendon Street, Oxford OX2 6DP

Oxford University Press is a department of the University of Oxford.
It furthers the University's objective of excellence in research, scholarship,
and education by publishing worldwide in

Oxford New York

Auckland Cape Town Dar es Salaam Hong Kong Karachi
Kuala Lumpur Madrid Melbourne Mexico City Nairobi
New Delhi Shanghai Taipei Toronto

With offices in
Argentina Austria Brazil Chile Czech Republic France Greece
Guatemala Hungary Italy Japan Poland Portugal Singapore
South Korea Switzerland Thailand Turkey Ukraine Vietnam

British Library Cataloguing in Publication Data available

ISBN: 978-0-19-273872-1 (hardback)
ISBN: 978-0-19-273873-8 (paperback)
ISBN: 978-0-19-273874-5 (paperback with audio CD)

2 4 6 8 10 9 7 5 3

Printed in China

Paper used in the production of this book is a natural, recyclable product made
from wood grown in sustainable forests. The manufacturing process conforms
to the environmental regulations of the country of origin

Thanks to Anderson, Wilder, and Schuyler Daffey
for the framed robot drawing in Winnie's kitchen.
The illustration helped raise funds for the Art Room—K.P.

www.winnie-the-witch.com

Valerie Thomas and Korky Paul

Winnie's Big Bad Robot

OXFORD

UNIVERSITY PRESS

Every Wednesday afternoon Winnie the Witch and her big black cat Wilbur went to art classes in the library.

They learned how to paint
and draw, knit and sew,
make pots and posters,
and lots of other things.
Winnie the Witch really
enjoyed *all* of the classes.

Wilbur enjoyed *some* of them.

This Wednesday they were making models.
Winnie decided to make a bear.

She chose a cardboard box for the head.

She glued on the eyes, nose, and mouth.

Then she made the body,

arms,

and legs.

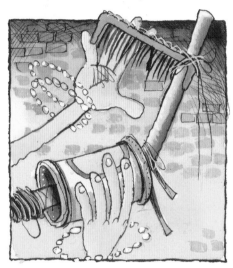

It looked good. The teacher liked it too.

'That's a lovely robot you've
made, Winnie,' she said.
Winnie was cross. *A robot?*

But when she looked at it carefully,
it did look a bit like a robot.
Everybody admired it.

Winnie sat the robot on her broomstick.
Then Winnie, Wilbur, and the robot flew home.

Winnie stood the robot on the kitchen table.
'It's a pity it's not a real robot,' she said.

Then Winnie had an idea.
She picked up her magic
wand, shouted,

Abracadabra!

. . . and there in the kitchen was a real robot.
'Beep, beep, beep,' said the robot.
Its eyes flashed red and green.

Winnie was delighted.
'Isn't this a lovely robot, Wilbur?' Winnie said.

Wilbur didn't think so.
The robot walked over to
Wilbur and pulled his tail.
'Yeeoww!' cried Wilbur.

'Naughty robot!' Winnie said.
'You mustn't pull poor Wilbur's tail!'

The robot looked at Winnie.
Then it leaned over and pinched her nose.
'Oww!' said Winnie. 'That hurt.
I've made a bad robot, Wilbur.
I'll change it back into a model.'

Winnie went to pick up her magic wand.
But the robot was too fast for her.

It grabbed
Winnie's wand,

walked up the wall,

across the ceiling,

and then out of the window.

'Oh no!' shouted Winnie.
'My wand still has the robot spell on it, Wilbur.
We have to get it back.'

Winnie and Wilbur tiptoed
out of the front door.
They hid behind the tallest tree.

The big bad robot
was waving Winnie's wand.

Two robot frogs jumped into the pond.
Three robot ducks flew across the sky.
The robot waved the wand again and
four robot rabbits hopped across the grass.

Then the robot waved the wand
at Winnie's front door . . .

and there was an enormous robot house.

Winnie waited
until the robot
walked past the tree.

She jumped out,

'Blithering
broomsticks!'
Winnie whispered.
'My lovely house is
a robot house!
We have to get my
wand back, Wilbur.'

and Winnie the Witch was Winnie the Robot.

Oh no!

Winnie the Robot walked round and round the garden.
'**Beep, beep, beep,**' she said.

'**Meeoow!**' said Wilbur.
He didn't like Winnie the Robot.
He wanted Winnie the Witch back again.
He would have to get Winnie's wand.

But how?

Wilbur had an excellent idea.

He grabbed a creeper . . .

swung out over the big
bad robot, and snatched
Winnie's wand.

Then he swung across to Winnie the Robot,

and
dropped
the
wand
into
her
hand.

Winnie the Robot waved the wand
again and again, and shouted

Abra-beep-beep-cadabra . . .

Two frogs jumped into the pond,
three ducks flew up into the sky,
four rabbits hopped across the grass,
the robot house was Winnie's house,
Winnie the Robot was Winnie the Witch,
and instead of a big bad robot there was
a little pile of junk.

Winnie the Witch flopped down
into her deckchair.
Wilbur curled up in her lap.

'Thank you, Wilbur,' Winnie said.
'I am very lucky to have such a clever cat.'
'**Purr, purr, purr,**' said Wilbur.